Free!

GREAT ESCAPES FROM SLAVERY ON THE UNDERGROUND RAILROAD

BASED ON TRUE STORIES

BY
LORENE CARY

New City Community Press
Third World Press
ISBN:0-88378-268-5
Design by Jaeyun Jung
Cover and illustrations by Beth Lewis

Third World Press provides quality literature that primarily focuses on issues, themes, and critique related to an African American public. The Third World Press mission is to make this literature accessible to as many individuals as possible including our targeted market of primarily African American readers.

The Third World Press mission to provide quality literature is further enhanced by our marketing goals to increase the overall awareness for the titles that we publish, and to expand beyond our current customer base of predominately African American readers, who are generally identified as college-educated and moderately affluent. These readers are consistent book-purchasing clients with academic or scholarly affiliation. Our goals are to cultivate a broader readership of individuals who want to gain greater insight into African American cultural traditions; to reach individuals that are younger and/or less scholarly-focused; and also to reach that customer who just did not know that we existed.

Third World Press
P. O. Box 19730
7822 S. Dobson Ave.
Chicago, IL 60619
Tel: 773.651.0700
Fax: 773.651.7286
Email: twpress3@aol.com

New City Community Press is grounded in the belief that writing is
an implicit organizing tool that can produce social change. We imagine
writing as an act that can project us beyond the parameters of individual
selfhood into the body politic. To that end, New City works with communities struggling to gain cultural and political representation, aiding
them in recording and distributing their stories to the larger public. We
believe that through the inclusion of these voices into daily life, alterna-
tive ways of speaking, writing, and communicating manifest themselves,
ultimately reenvisioning the promise of community.

New City Community Press
7715 Crittenden St. #222
Philadelphia, PA 19118
Tel: 215.204.7347
Email: Sjparks@syr.edu
Web: www.newcitypress.org

Executive Director: Stephen Parks, Syracuse University
Editor: August Tarrier, University of Baltimore

Publications

Chinatown Live(s): Oral Histories from Philadelphia's Chinatown

*Espejos y Ventanas/Mirrors and Windows: Oral Histories of Mexican
Farmworkers and Their Families*

No Restraints: An Anthology of Disability Cullture in Philadelphia

Nourish Your Soul: A Community Cookbook

The Forgotten Bottom Remembered: Stories from a Philadelphia Neighborhood

Open City: A Journal of Community Arts and Culture (Vols. 1 and 2)

CONTENTS

∿∿∿

ACKNOWLEDGEMENTS

⩗⩗⩗⩗

Thanks to Phil Lapsansky of the Library Company of Philadelphia for introducing me to William Still and his book, and to Millicent Sparks of the Civil War and Underground Railroad Museum of Philadelphia for corrections. I am also grateful to Nancy Hickman for editing and research and to Avi Alpert for last-minute fact-checking.

Thanks to the Springside School lower school teachers who insisted that I collect and publish these stories, years after two Greenfield School teachers, Ms. Weil and Mrs. Mann, welcomed me into their classrooms to try them out. Their students' enthusiastic improvisation—vying to tape each other into a U-Haul box to imagine the girl who mailed herself north—showed me how poorly we document African-American *agency* in history and how hungry children are to experience the support that the ancestors' intelligence, force, and tenacity provides, if only we know it.

Thanks to my mother, Carole J. Cary, for loving Jane Johnson as much as I do, and to my husband, The Rev. Robert Smith, who continues to urge me toward the courage of my obsessions, and who directed first- and second-grade *Free!* improvs with bonnets, hobby horses, repeated requests of "Can I go to the bathroom?"—the works.

Thanks to advance-copy youth readers, especially Katie and Hilary Sugg, and young editor Sara Bourgeau; also, the Shute family.

I am indebted to Beth Lewis for updating nineteenth-century pen-and-ink drawings into fresh new images of timeless liberation and life force.

Thanks to Haki Madhubuti and Bennett Johnson of Third World Press and Dr. Steve Parks, August Tarrier, and Nicole Meyenberg of New City Community Press, who've created a unique business model of joint publication, and to Michael Bourret and Jane Dystel of Dystel and Goderich for helping to make it happen.

Thank you, daughters Laura Hagans Smith and Zoë Drayton Smith, for reading, acting out, and responding to these stories as I was collecting them. Now we'll hand them, with love, to future readers, including, especially, Jordan Miller and Jessica Hugee, Samantha and Zachary Smith, and Joshua and Coleman Hopson, just in case you need to grab something off the shelf one night—*quick!*—for an emergency book report. 🔲

INTRODUCTION

I wrote these stories because they are test cases of American freedom—and deeply affecting human stories about hope and struggle. They are stories I wanted my children to know, and that I wanted to know myself as a child. Slavery was not a standard curriculum item like Indians and Pilgrims, in whose honor we made hats to wear home at dismissal. (*"Two rows, boys and girls, line up; nobody moves until we have silence."*) But freedom was part of the curriculum, and the history of Africans in America running to freedom and walking, mailing themselves, riding, stowing away, rowing and sailing, tells us how desperately the human spirit hungers for freedom—as well as for dominance over others.

At some point in second grade, we touched on the subject. The moment I have locked in memory stands out as clearly as the rest of the year's slide-projection images: the radio on the counter announcing that President Kennedy had been shot; my friend Marlon standing at the back of the room for punishment with his arms outstretched until they ached; the faint, ineradicable scent of bergamot oil and urine that clung to the chair of the accident-prone girl who sat in front of me.

I wanted to know more about the enslaved black people. How did they live? What did they eat? What happened when they refused to work? Did they try to escape? What happened to the children? Who beat whom? What was it like? How did it end? Popular culture had planted *Gone with the Wind* images in my head. Now I wanted proper school facts to educate my imagination, which was thin and useless about these ancestors.

I wanted to know more about the enslaved black people. How did they live? What did they eat? What happened when they refused to work?

But there weren't any facts. Our teacher told us that. Almost none at all. The problem was that the slavery had happened far away in the South, that most blacks had been illiterate, and that they *had left very few records*. She wished she could tell us, but nobody knew. Too bad. What a shame.

My cheeks burned each time I remembered. It was like having relatives who hadn't paid the rent and had gotten themselves evicted from history. Now we couldn't find them—no forwarding address, no phone.

A dozen years later at the University of Pennsylvania, Professor Houston A. Baker, Jr., quoted Thomas Jefferson's *Notes on the State of Virginia* and challenged us students to find better histories for ourselves than we'd inherited. Jefferson knew, he said, that if black people remembered America's injuries, they would never live in peace with their white neighbors. Our culture colludes in the forgetting. It helps keep the peace.

But records do exist, of course, and first-person narratives and eyewitness accounts; there are maps and letters and accounts and lists, daguerreotypes, sketches, material objects (beautifully reproduced in the breathtaking book *Lest I Forget*). In my hometown, Philadelphia, nearly *everybody* involved left records. Philadelphia sheltered one of the largest free black populations in the U.S. in the antebellum years. It was home to those notorious record-keeping Quakers and the indefatigable William Still, co-chair of the Vigilance Committee of the Pennsylvania Committee for the Abolition of Slavery. Of all the books I discovered while writing *The Price of a Child*, the one that showed most brilliantly the desperate insistence of the fugitives, the diversity of their methods, and the size of the community that supported them was *The Underground Railroad*, self-published in 1872 by William Still.

So compelling were these escapes that I began to tell them to my own children, including the story of Jane Johnson on which *The Price of a Child* is based. (As part of the **One Book, One Philadelphia** program for 2003, this story was featured on the Free Library of Philadelphia website and published in *The Philadelphia Inquirer* Sunday magazine, so that young children and beginner-reader adults could read

Jane Johnson's story while the rest of the city read *The Price of a Child*.) I wanted my girls to know more than their schools were teaching them and I wanted them to learn about slavery not from some fictional observer, but from the very people who risked their lives and sacrificed family, safety, and health to be free. A few times over the years, my husband and I visited our daughters' classrooms, not only to tell the stories, but to lead the children in acting them out in spirited improvisations to which the children brought their own inventiveness and open hearts.

I chose stories with mostly successful endings and not-too-intense passages, a balance of male-female, and a variety of escape strategies that use wit, courage, sheer physical power, will, cunning—and outrageous hope. They allow our twenty-first-century minds *to imagine actively* the inner lives of enslaved people—and put ourselves in their places, not with shame, but with compassion and respect.

When I wrote the stories to send home so that parents and children could read them together, I realized that I wanted to find language that would be simple and compelling, capable of holding complex meaning—as well as satisfying to the more mature reader of any literacy level. This collection is the result of that project. It begins with the astonishing story of the escape that led William's own brother, Peter Still, born a slave, to William Still's door. Because William knew firsthand the pain of separation from family and the joy of reunion, he decided to keep track of every escape he could. The other stories are those that create loop tapes in the imagination: a pregnant young woman mailed north in a box, a girl who dresses as a boy to avoid detection, a man riding a horse half a mile across the churning Potomac River.

They allow our twenty-first-century minds *to imagine actively* the inner lives of enslaved people— and put ourselves in their places, not with shame, but with compassion and respect.

Regarding historical accuracy, I've used the same principles I did in my adult book to write these stories. That is, I have not made up any action for the very real people described here. Everything that they do or say is what William Still recorded: things he saw himself, the testimony or letters of participants, or newspaper accounts. I have tried to tell the stories with a resonant clarity, avoiding the disrespectful practice of inserting thoughts into the characters' heads.

For me and for my children, these are texts that teach liberation. They get us in close to ultimate acts of resistance, where individuals overcome their own fear as well as the failings of their country's political vision. There should be no diminishment of the fact of slavery here, no pabulum or condescension. When people go underground, they must face down their own terror, as well as traps set for them by their fellows. We go with these people inside the box, under the burlap sack, on the saddle, clinging to the horse's mane as we plunge across the freezing river. We know the burden of enslavement because we see the desperate insistence of the escape from it.

These fugitives, running for their own freedom, became a significant economic and political force in antebellum history. In their time, tens of thousands of individual revolts were hushed and covered up. By telling these stories now, we honor the extravagant cost these people paid to amend our democracy. And by paying attention to how these Americans made a way out of no way, we tutor our children and ourselves in political action and hope. 🗔

∿∿∿

We go with these people inside the box, under the burlap sack, on the saddle, clinging to the horse's mane as we plunge across the freezing river.

∿∿∿

William

&

Peter Still

"I AM YOUR BROTHER"

Wentworth Still wrote a book about the Underground Railroad—that's because his own family struggled so hard for freedom.

His father, Levin Still, worked nights—after working all day for his master—to earn enough money to buy himself out of slavery in Maryland. The Stills could only earn enough to buy Levin out, so he had to leave his family, a wife and four children. He planned to establish himself in the North and then go back for them. But his wife, Cydney, didn't wait.

Instead, she ran away with all four children. Levin had been successful, after all, and Cydney thought she could make it, too. But an escaped mother with four children could only run so fast; and the distinctive family group could be recognized by anyone who could read the papers. They were caught—and returned.

~~~~~

Their grandmother told them that their parents had taken their sisters to Philadelphia, a name they'd never forget.

~~~~~

The next time Cydney ran away from Maryland, she only took the two younger children, two daughters. She left the two boys, hoping that boys could take care of themselves in their parents' absence, and that their grandmother, who was still there, would watch over them with love. Peter and Levin Still were six and eight years old. Soon afterward, the man who owned them sold the boys south to another farmer, far away in Alabama.

The boys were so young that they didn't know exactly what had happened to them. Their grandmother told them that their parents had taken their sisters to Philadelphia, a name they'd never forget. They didn't know that their mother and sisters had walked all night for several weeks; that they slept during the daytime wherever they could, sometimes in the houses of people who knew that slavery was wrong. They didn't know how hungry their mother and sisters were. They didn't know that one sister was too small and tired to go farther, so their mother found a kind family who was willing to keep her until they were able to get all the way north to Levin Still, who went back to get her. They didn't know that when she became free, their mother changed her name to Charity to avoid capture.

Levin died when he was a young man. The younger brother, Peter, promised himself and his wife and his own children that one day he too would get free—and find his parents.
When he was a grown man, Peter did just what his own father had done: he worked at every odd job he could find, and worked with his wife at night throughout his adulthood for about 20 years until they'd made enough money to buy his own freedom. Then, no doubt telling his own wife as his father had told his mother, that he was going on ahead to make a place for them, he went north to Philadelphia to look for his parents.

One of the first people he met in Philadelphia was William Still, his brother, born free in New Jersey, now a grown man. William worked as a clerk in the anti-slavery office at 5th and Arch Streets, but at night and on the weekends, he helped runaway slaves get free. He was what they called a Vigilance man.

William has written in his book how Peter came up to him in his shop in Philadelphia. He told William his name and he said, "I am looking for my family. I know that my mother is named Cydney and my father is named Levin, but I do not know their last names."
William couldn't believe it. All he could say at first was: "I am your brother."

~~~~~~

William couldn't believe it. All he could say at first was: "I am your brother."

~~~~~~

This experience changed William's life. He decided not only to help people escape from slavery, but also to keep careful records of who'd been through Philadelphia seeking freedom. Who could tell, he wrote, when families might need help to find their loved ones? Now, more than 130 years later, we can learn these stories, thanks to William Still. ▣

"I Want My Freedom"

Jane Johnson's Escape with
the Philadelphia Vigilance
Committee, 1855 .

At 4:30 in the afternoon on Wednesday, the 25th of July, 1855, an out-of-breath boy brought the following note to William Still's Philadelphia office:

Mr. Still—SIR—: Will you come down to Bloodgood's Hotel as soon as possible—as there are three fugitive slaves here and they want liberty. Their master is here with them on his way to New York.

The boy had run, excited and scared, carrying the message about a woman named Jane Johnson, who had asked first one, then another, of the black workers at Bloodgood's to help her and her two children to escape. They'd come up from Virginia, and this short layover in Philadelphia seemed her best chance—maybe her only chance—for freedom.

Even while she was asking for help, however, she agonized. Although she'd convinced her master, Col. Wheeler, to let her bring two children along, he'd insisted that she leave her third child, a baby, behind in Virginia. She suspected that he'd done it to keep her from trying to escape. She also suspected that he and his wife were planning to sell the baby while she was away.

William Still read the letter and strode the few blocks to the office of his Underground Railroad partner, Passmore Williamson. William and Passmore led the Philadelphia Vigilance Committee, a group of people who stayed alert and *vigilant* to rescue escaping people coming through Philadelphia. At first Passmore said that he'd go through with business he'd scheduled that would take him to Harrisburg that night, but then, after William Still left, Passmore changed his mind. He sent a telegram to cancel his meeting, and ran to catch up with William. Together, the two men hurried to the hotel.

But "the three fugitives"—Jane Johnson and her two children—had already left. Their master had taken them to the ferryboat to Camden, NJ, to catch the New York train. So William and Passmore rushed to Dock Street, hoping to intercept the ferry before it pushed off.

There, on the upper deck, they saw her: a tall woman with two children, sitting next to her master, and looking nervously over the heads of the people on the boat as if she were expecting someone. The Vigilance men went up the steps. William walked straight to the woman and spoke to her directly. He didn't even know her name.

"Are you traveling?" he asked.
"Yes," she answered.
"With whom?"

She nodded toward the man sitting next to her. In response, the master fidgeted in his seat and said something into her ear.

William turned to the man. "Do they belong to you, Sir?"
"Yes," he answered. "They are in my charge."

While they were talking, Passmore used his eyes to beckon five African-American porters who were working on the pier to come up to the second deck of the ferryboat. It looked as if he and his partner were going to need help.

Quietly, almost so no one noticed, the porters worked their way toward the conflict. Passmore and William checked each other's eyes and nodded. Then, William Still spoke to Jane Johnson in a bold, commanding voice, almost as if he were making a *speech* to the entire ferryboat and the crowd of workers who were gathering to watch from the dock. "You are entitled to your freedom according to the laws of Pennsylvania, having been brought into the state by your owner."

The master broke in: "She understands all the laws."

But William would not be stopped. "If you prefer freedom to

slavery, as we suppose everybody does, you have the chance to accept it now."

"Of *course,* she's free to leave if she chooses," the master interrupted, "but she's visiting friends in New York." That wasn't true. They were really going to New York to catch a boat to Nicaragua, where the master would work for the U.S. government. Jane didn't know anyone there.

"Act calmly," William Still continued, "Don't be frightened by your master—you are as much entitled to your freedom as we are, *or as he is—*"

"Act calmly," William Still continued, "Don't be frightened by your master—you are as much entitled to your freedom as we are, *or as he is—*"

"She's left other children in Virginia," the master warned, "from whom it would be hard, *so hard,* to separate her." (He was referring to her baby, whom he *had* already made plans to sell.)

Other passengers began to shout their encouragement and opinions. One man told the Vigilance men to leave them alone, because Jane and her children were the master's property. Others disagreed; they told Jane to go with Still and Williamson—go while she had a chance.

"Be determined," William continued, "and *you will be* protected by the law." (He meant Pennsylvania law. The United States Federal law did not protect her; in fact, U.S. law promised to return people who escaped—and even hired marshals and slave catchers to hunt them down.)

Finally, Jane Johnson spoke: "*I am not free,*" she said. "*But I want my freedom. I always wanted to be free, but he holds me.*"

"She *is* free," the master yelled. "I was going to give her her freedom—"

The bell rang for the ferryboat. In a moment, it would leave.

William touched Jane's arm. "Come," he said.
"Go along; go along," said someone behind her.

Then it began, first in a simple action of resistance: Jane stood. Then began the confusion. Jane's older son stood alongside her, knowing full well the audacity and danger of his mother's stand. He pulled his younger brother's hand.

~~~~~

Finally, Jane Johnson spoke: "*I am not free,*" she said. "*But I want my freedom. I always wanted to be free, but he holds me.*"

~~~~~

Then Wheeler, the master, jumped up and tried to hold her back. The porters—whom Passmore had motioned to stand guard—held Wheeler while Jane took William Still's hand and Passmore helped the children. The seven-year-old became so frightened that he began to cry and another passenger had to help carry him off.

Other ferryboat passengers stood, a crowd gathered and someone, referring to the master, hollered out, "Knock him down, knock him down!"

But the Vigilance men and the porters resisted any violence they might have felt. They resisted the violence of his ownership and the laws that made some Americans more powerful and more human than others. And despite her shouting master and crying son, despite the baby left behind in Virginia and the grief that threatened to close like a curtain over any hope of future joy, Jane walked with utter determination—off the ferry and into a carriage that took her away to freedom. ◩

CROSSING THE RIVER ON HORSEBACK IN THE NIGHT

Dismal. On Christmas night, 1856, Robert Brown left Martinsburg, Virginia, in the cold dark, in freezing rain. His mind and heart were dismal, too, frozen underneath a low-slung sky stained purple with grief.

Just five days before, Mrs. Brown and their four children had been sold by a master who was angry with her. Robert was crazy with trying to find a solution. He had found a buyer in the county, and he had told the master, so that even if his family were separated, he would still be able to visit them. But the Browns' master was so angry that he would only sell them to someone who lived far away. Robert Brown could not find or follow them. His family was split apart. Brimming with sadness and rage, Robert Brown stole a horse and galloped north.

∿∿∿

At the Potomac River, he and the horse plunged into the water.

∿∿∿

At the Potomac River, he and the horse plunged into the water. Strong and game, the horse began to swim. The river spread out for half a mile—*half a mile* of cold, rushing water. The horse pumped his legs. Robert hung on against the drag and pull of the tide; his clothes froze to his skin. He wrapped the reins around his hands and dug his fingertips into the mane. He squeezed the flanks with his knees and lay his body close along the horse's neck to keep from being washed off the saddle. Together, Robert and the horse stroked to the other bank.

Then, as Christmas night wore on toward a swollen, wet, gray morning, Robert Brown rode another 40 miles along the muddy roads. When the courageous horse gave out, Robert tied him to a fencepost, and walked on.

For two days, he dared not talk to anyone for fear of being arrested. So he walked on, driving himself as he'd driven the horse: *Walk on.*

He walked on despite the cold and without any food. *Walk on.*

He arrived in Philadelphia a few hours before dawn on New Year's morning, carrying inside his coat a picture of his dear wife, and small fuzzy locks of black hair, wrapped in thin scraps of fabric, from his four children. He knew each lock, one from the other.

For two days, he dared not talk to anyone for fear of being arrested. So he walked on, driving himself as he'd driven the horse: *Walk on.*

WILLIAM AND ELLEN CRAFT

African-Americans come in all colors. Some enslaved people who looked white used their skin color to aid them in their escape. That's what Ellen Craft did when she and her husband William planned their getaway.

Before they left Georgia, William cut Ellen's hair and outfitted her in men's clothing: a black suit and cloak and high-heeled boots.

Since they knew that their owner would soon post an advertisement, and since it was dangerous for them to be seen traveling together, they disguised Ellen as a young master planter—with William pretending to be her servant.

Before they left Georgia, William cut Ellen's hair and outfitted her in men's clothing: a black suit and cloak and high-heeled boots. But she didn't look quite manly enough; for one thing, her face was too smooth. And when they'd need to spend the night in hotels, Ellen would be unable to write her fake name in the register book, because, as a slave, she was not allowed to learn to read and write.

So they decided to make her up as a *sickly* young man, almost an invalid. They'd pretend that he could only get around with the careful help of his servant, William. They wrapped Ellen's neck and jaw in a muffler to cover her beardless chin, as if she had a sore tooth or jaw; they hung her right arm in a sling so that she *couldn't* write; they put thick green spectacles on her face so that it appeared she couldn't see well; and they gave her a cane to lean on. When someone spoke to the two of them, Ellen leaned in toward William, and he repeated what had been said into her ear, as if she were hard of hearing.

In this way they traveled north on the "cars," as they called rail-road trains then, riding all day without a problem, and stopping at hotels at night. The charade fooled everyone.

In Baltimore, though, just a few hours from freedom, they ran into trouble. At the ticket window, William asked for tickets for himself and his "master." But the man would not sell them to him. Enslaved people had to have special papers, he said, and without them, William could not buy a ticket or ride the train. Period.

 William thought fast, very fast. He said that he didn't know anything about the rules, but that his young master was sick and had to get to Philadelphia immediately for medical treatment. Instead of pleading, William Craft insisted, as if this man's quibbling would jeopardize the young planter's life.

"My master," he said simply, "can*not* be detained."

The ticket master had little choice but to give in—and William and Ellen Craft took their final ride to freedom. That day they arrived in Philadelphia.

Soon after, they settled in Boston, but when two slave catchers were issued warrants for their arrest, William and Ellen left the U.S. for England. There, they raised a family and wrote their story.

William thought fast, very fast. He said that he didn't know anything about the rules, but that his young master was sick and had to get to Philadelphia immediately for medical treatment.

HIDING BELOW DECK

A SPRAY OF SPLINTERS

"IF YOU

SPLINTERS AXE

WANT TO

SEARCH"

Captain F. was rough-spoken and middle-aged, a white sea captain who was not only hard to read, but hard. Sea captains had to be hard. They managed crews of hard men who settled arguments with fists and knives. And they had to be alert every minute to pilot wooden boats through storms, wind, hurricanes, and treacherous tides. Captain F. looked the part; he had a big, stern face made leathery by the sun, and heavy brows over cloudy eyes that revealed nothing of what was going on in his mind. He kept a cool head under pressure—and he kept his secrets, including the dangerous fact that he was a friend to black fugitives.

Captain F. called on all his skills in November, 1855. The mayor of Norfolk, Virginia brought a posse of deputies armed with axes and spears to his schooner, which was loaded with wheat and ready to sail. Rumor had it that more than 20 people had escaped in the past few days, and search posses had been raking the land for them. Now the mayor's attention turned toward the port. A docked boat was a perfect hideaway—and, the mayor added meaningfully, he had reason to suspect this one.

"Well," said Captain F. casually. "Here I am, and this is my boat. Go ahead and search."

And they did, clumsily, but with gusto. The deputies used their long-handled spears to stab into the bales of wheat. They plunged the blades in deep. The wheat did not bleed or groan, however, so that the mayor decided after some time that he was "barking up the wrong tree."

"Well," said Captain F. casually. "Here I am, and this is my boat. Go ahead and search."

Instead, he directed the men to chop through the deck, and the destruction began again. They hacked, expecting to hit human flesh, but the below-deck hiding places were too cleverly made to be discovered right away by the careless deputies. But if they kept at it, the captain knew, eventually they would hit someone.

~~~~~

He raised the axe above his head, and in one huge, startling movement, sliced into the deck to send a spray of splinters flying.

~~~~~

So he made his move. As if he had lost patience with them, Captain F. worked his eyebrows up and down in his big, leathery face and said to the mayor, "Look here. I've stood still long enough while my boat has been damaged and chopped up."

The men stopped flailing as the ferocious-looking captain strode to the middle of the deck. "Now, if you want to search," he growled, and with his great, strong arms he grabbed an axe from the mayor's hand, "*if you want to search*, give me the axe, and then point out the spot you want opened and I'll open it for you *very quick*."

He raised the axe above his head, and in one huge, startling movement, sliced into the deck to send a spray of splinters flying.

 Captain F. knew something about axes and ships' decks. He also knew that he was putting on a freedom theater right there in their faces and that he'd have to be convincing. He knew that the people hiding below deck had to have nerves of steel and desperate discipline to stay silent despite the murderous chopping just above their heads. His thundering voice would give them encouragement even as it struck the deputies through with sudden fear.

He knew that the people hiding below deck had to have nerves of steel and desperate discipline to stay silent despite the murderous chopping just above their heads.

〜〜〜

Captain F. stomped to another place on deck he knew to be safe. "*I said*: Tell me where. You want to open this up? I'll open it for you. . . ." Once again he raised the axe, letting the weight of it balance for a moment above his head, menacing. These men were bullies; Captain F. had seen bullies all his life. They carried fear inside them and quieted it with their own violence. Hunting for fugitives made them feel larger than they were. Now that the captain had taken charge, with his bellowing voice smacking at them like the surf, and splinters whizzing past their faces, the fear inside awoke. Unsure of what to do next, they looked to the mayor.

"All right, all right," said the mayor, as if *he* were in control. "We're finished here."

The mayor directed one of his posse to give the captain five dollars, which Virginia law promised to every ship that was searched. Five dollars would not begin to pay what it would cost to repair the damage to Captain F.'s deck, but he needed to get out of there, and didn't want to risk taking the time to argue. Twenty-one people huddled in the dark compartments in the ship's belly were depending on his continued good judgment.

They dared not move until they docked in Philadelphia. Once there, and once the ship was unloaded and "empty," the secret passengers were finally able to step out onto dry land. Fifteen men and five women were sent on to freedom further north. One fugitive, who was sick to begin with, made it to Philadelphia, but no further.

And Captain F. sailed south again, to pick up more precious cargo. ◫

CHARLES GILBERT

RUNAWAY

"Open up!"

Old Point Comfort

COMFORT

RUNAWAY

Charles Gilbert was a young man with a smooth face and a busy mind. And he never gave up. In 1854 Charles was owned by a man named Benjamin Davis in Richmond, Virginia. Davis was a trader; he made his living from selling people. Charles was smart, young, good-looking and strong, but for some reason Davis couldn't seem to sell him right away. Maybe buyers could sense that they'd lose their investment to freedom. In any event, Charles used the time to figure.

He figured that a boat headed north would be as good a way out as any, and he found out that the captain of a Boston schooner might be approachable. Somehow Charles got word to the captain, who made a deal. If Charles could scrape together ten dollars, and if he could get himself to Old Point Comfort, 160 miles away, the captain would let Charles onto the boat and keep quiet about it.

A hundred and sixty miles for a fugitive without papers was daunting, but Charles knew the way: he'd grown up in Old Point Comfort. The place wasn't home really, and certainly not comfortable for African-Americans, but his mother and brothers lived there, and old, dear friends. The fact was, though, that they made Comfort even *more* dangerous for Charles than other towns. Once Davis the trader put an ad into the newspapers announcing that Charles had escaped and describing what he looked like, Old Point Comfort was the first place slave catchers went to look. If they caught him, Davis the trader would pay $200. Later the number grew to $550, about $12,200 in today's money.

Not only was it dangerous for Charles, it was just as dangerous for his loved ones—maybe more so. If a free person in Virginia was discovered helping fugitives, the courts could require him or her to pay a fine. The fines were too large for a working person to pay. Then the courts could force the accused person to sell his or her house, or land or belongings to meet the payment. Free black people could legally be captured and sold *into slavery* to raise enough money to pay off their debt. People who were already in bondage could be beaten for the crime of aiding a fugitive—and then sold away from *their* loved ones.

So when he arrived at the port that he could well have called *No* Comfort, crawling with slave-hunters, stayed away from his family and friends. He gave up on the idea of getting to the Boston schooner. Now that he'd been advertised, anyone could recognize him. He knew that many citizens were in the habit of reading runaway ads very carefully. For them, turning in someone like Charles for $200, $300, or $500 would be like finding money in the road. He dared not even visit his mother, although they exchanged words through a friend. And although Charles didn't know it, his mother was working to find alternatives. The Boston boat hadn't worked, but they lived near a port. There were other boats, maybe even other helpful captains.

After staying with one friend for a week, and realizing the danger his friend was in for helping him, Charles Gilbert was determined to find a place to hide until he could figure out his next move. And the next and the next . . . .

᠕᠊᠕᠊᠕᠊

It must have taken great discipline for Charles Gilbert, an active young man with an active mind, to stay curled up, still, and alone every day. He did it for four weeks.

᠕᠊᠕᠊᠕᠊

He remembered the large Higee Hotel in the neighborhood—it stood three feet off the ground on big wooden pillars. Charles crawled under and hid himself in a dark, gloomy corner near the cistern tank where the hotel stored water. It must have taken great discipline for Charles Gilbert, an active young man with an active mind, to stay curled up, still, and alone every day. He did it for four weeks. Only at night would he crawl out from under the Higee, stretch his cramped body in the moonlight and scrounge for food. Usually, he made his daily meal by picking through leftovers that the cook threw into a slop tub for the hogs. He was a slim, smooth-faced young man who grew slimmer, more serious, and more silent. He was an inventive young man trying to invent freedom.

One evening, he heard a boy approaching—under the hotel. Charles could hear the boy talking in a musical Irish accent to his father, who walked upright next to the building. They were hunting runaway chickens for dinner. The hotel was a big building, but the boy was coming directly to the dark corner where Charles had made his hideout. Almost faster than he could think, Charles came upon an idea: he made a sound like the bark of a savage dog, the kind that had gotten away from an owner and now ran wild. He followed the bark with a snarl and a low growl that rolled around in his chest and caught in his throat.

It worked. The boy scrambled, terrified, out from under the hotel. But his father also heard Charles' growls, and swore that he'd return later with his gun and shoot the dog that had threatened his son—and might well be rabid.

That night, before the man returned, Charles left his hiding place and went into the woods in an area away from the Port. He hid in the woods for a day, but was not satisfied with its safety. So he climbed an oak tree and lay in its large upper branches trying to figure what to do next. He still didn't dare put his family in danger, but he thought of a friend, Isabella, whom the slave traders might not know he knew.

~~~~~

When Charles Gilbert showed up at her door, thin and dirty and tired, she took him in immediately and gave him food and friendship. But she couldn't think of what to do to keep him hidden.

~~~~~

Isabella was a washerwoman, a free black woman who used her house as a place to wash clothes for other people. Some people dropped off their dirty clothes to her, the way we take clothes to the cleaners, and in some cases, she went to their houses, picked up their clothes, washed them at her place, and then took them back. To make the business work, she had to handle whole hillsides of dirty laundry each week. She washed the clothes by hand in water she heated over the fire, with soap she made herself from fat and lye and ashes. She dried them outside on clotheslines and ironed them indoors with starch broken off from big white chunks and dissolved in water. It was hot, hard, backbreaking and hand-destroying work and she couldn't do it all alone. Isabella paid other young women to work with her. Sometimes they'd live in the upstairs; the downstairs was all taken up with piles of wash. Isabella was smart and tough. She was a hard worker and a good friend. When Charles Gilbert showed up at her door, thin and dirty and tired, she took him in immediately and gave him food and friendship. But she couldn't think of what to do to keep him hidden.

Charles, however, who'd spent a month on the run, had thought of nothing *but* hiding. While hotel guests and workers had been about their work, he'd lived *under* them. He'd dreamt of hiding in the boat, under the deck. Even his life in slavery had been lived under the active free life where other Americans bought land, built houses, and made money—from slaves' work—to take care of their families. Underneath was unpleasant and damp and mean, but one could stay alive for a while, like a mushroom, quiet and undiscovered. He found a place in Isabella's house where the floorboards were built over a shallow crawl space. With another friend, John Thomas, Isabella and Charles pried up the board, and the thin young Charles turned sideways to slip his body in before lying down. Then Isabella lay the board back in its place, replaced the nails in their holes and went about her business as if no one were there. Charles stayed under the floor, warmed by friendly sounds, and had regular meals and exercise at night, when the household was asleep and it was safe to move around.

~~~~

With another friend, John Thomas, Isabella and Charles pried up the board, and the thin young Charles turned sideways to slip his body in before lying down.

~~~~

Then, in two weeks, the slave hunters and police arrived at the wash-house. They demanded to come in. Charles heard their heavy boots and voices asking about him. Isabella said she knew nothing. They offered Isabella and a friend $25 if they'd give them a clue to point them toward Charles. Isabella and her friend said they knew nothing and the officers left. That night, so did Charles.

 The next two weeks were a blur: from airless crawl space under the Higee Hotel again to the woods. From the woods' thorny thickets to a buggy, boggy marsh, where every step sank his feet into stinking mud, where water rats and snakes skimmed and skittered through the rushes. Now, Charles had no plan, no back up, no ideas. Charles couldn't secure his passage to freedom now, and he couldn't even plan or figure. He could only just stay alive and out of the slave hunters' grasp.

But all the while Charles' mother had been busy. Working, working, working, she'd saved the $30 required for the captain of a steamer to Philadelphia to sneak Charles on. When word came, it came quickly. She sent someone to let Charles know that he had one day and night to get to the boat. Rejoicing, Charles returned to Isabella's wash-house. There, he'd be able to have a meal, wash, and know the time so that he'd be sure not to miss his chance. Charles' blood pumped fast.

In a few hours, however, the heavy boots of the officers strode up Isabella's steps. Their fists banged on her door. *Open up!* They wanted to know about her "boarders." Who was living here? Just the washer girls? No one else? No one?

One of the officers, without a word of warning or invitation, made his way up the stairs, right to the section of the house where Charles hid behind a curtain that the girls used to create a room divider to hang their clothes.

Charles had hidden and starved and run. He had put family and friends in danger. Now slavery remained as threatening as ever, as much a part of him as the terror it had taught him. Slavery was as close as the arrogant officer, who did not respect the privacy of Isabella's home, but walked right through it, prying. It was as close as the officer's hand that could grab Charles and take him back.

Slavery made Charles' skin into a prison. It made color into an illusion of inferiority, although Charles and Isabella and their families were born the equal of anyone—and forced to be cleverer and harder working than most. But since slavery had taught Charles that skin color was a mask that kept white people from seeing who he really was, he knew something that brought freedom up close, too—as close as hope. As close as the girl's dress lying near to hand.

As silently as the mushrooms that had grown on all the damp under-places where he'd kept himself alive, Charles slipped his thin body into one of the girls' dresses. Onto his head, he pulled one of their floppy calico bonnets, tying the trailers under the chin where his beard never had grown heavier than peach fuzz. The he stepped onto the other side of the curtain, where freedom was. He walked out of the room, past one officer. He walked downstairs, where the others stood questioning the dear Isabella, asking her the same questions over and over in the same insistent voices.

"Hey—"

Charles, dressed as a young woman, was heading for the door.

"Whose gal are you?" They assumed that she must belong to someone.
"Mr. Cockling's, sir," Charles said. He picked the name of a slaveholder nearby who had many slaves, too many for these men to recognize.
"What is your name?"
"Delie, sir."
"Go on, then," said the officer.
And he did, all the way to Philadelphia and beyond. ▣

Maria Weems Escaping as Jo Wright

Usually, the people in Philadelphia's Underground Railroad waited for escaped folks to come to them. As a rule, it was too dangerous for them to go south to get people out. But other times, sometimes—they heard of a person who needed help and was not able to sneak away. It happened with Maria Weems, a 10-year-old girl in Virginia. Three of her brothers had been sold away from the family. Her father was not with them. Her mother and sister had been bought out of slavery by a lawyer in Philadelphia who used his extra money to help people. After he bought them, he gave them their freedom, and they went to Canada.

To help Maria, the Underground Railroad folks called on a young white man who acted like a nineteenth-century spy. They'd nicknamed him Powder Boy when he had once smuggled enough gunpowder in the bottom of his boat to blow up an entire dock. Powder Boy loved danger and risk. He loved going into new cities, finding fugitive people, and helping them get out.

They'd nicknamed him Powder Boy when he had once smuggled enough gunpowder in the bottom of his boat to blow up an entire dock.

Maria Weems was exactly the sort of challenge that Powder Boy found exciting. The lawyer who had bought Maria's mother and sister and set them free gave Powder Boy the money he needed for travel and meals while he was on the road. Secretly, Powder Boy went to Richmond, Virginia, sneaked into the house, convinced young Maria that he was a friend, and transported her to Washington, D.C. But there they had to stop, because her former owners put ads in the newspapers announcing that she was missing. The ads gave her age, height, facial and body features, and it offered $500 to anyone who captured her and turned her in to her former owners. The Vigilance Committee decided that it was best for Powder Boy to leave her with the good people in Washington who had offered their house as a hideout. She had to *stay* hidden until they could figure a safe way to bring her north.

Meanwhile, another abolitionist, Dr. H., was preparing to ride from Philadelphia to Washington in a horse and buggy to fetch Maria, whose name was now "Jo Wright."

That was in the early fall. For the next month and a half, Maria prepared for the next part of her journey north. The people she was staying with helped, too. They began to dress her as a boy and teach her to look convincing. For the first time in her life she wore pantaloons, a boy's cap and jacket, and shoes. Meanwhile, another abolitionist, Dr. H., was preparing to ride from Philadelphia to Washington in a horse and buggy to fetch Maria, whose name was now "Jo Wright."

They arranged to meet in Washington, but not near any of the houses of the Vigilance Committee members. Instead they met right in front of The White House. When Dr. H. saw "Jo," he called to "him," and quickly, with ease and a "polite and natural manner," "Jo" jumped into the carriage and took the horse's reins and whip, while the doctor said goodbye to the lawyer and shook hands. Then the doctor got into the carriage and told "Jo" to "Drive on."

Pretending to be the doctor's stable and horse boy, "Jo" set the horse at a trot and headed north.

Once they were in the country, the doctor, who knew the horse better and knew the way, took over. To make sure that no one would suspect anything, Dr. H. spent the night with a slave-holding family he knew, making sure that "Jo" was given a quilt and pillow and kept next to his own bedroom for safety. The next day, the distinguished doctor and his "driver," headed for Pennsylvania.

There, William Still met "Jo," and said that he'd thought the doctor had been sent to bring back a young lady. Maria did not reply, because they were in a room full of people, and the doctor had told her not to tell who she was to anyone except Mr. Still. Still followed her outside, and when the two of them were alone, she said, "I am the one the doctor went after."

It was Thanksgiving Day, 1855. What a day of thanks it was for Maria and the Vigilance Committee!

Mr. Still congratulated her and helped send her to New York. The Vigilance people there moved her on to Canada, where she was reunited with her mother and sister.

This story doesn't end here, however. Maria's mother refused to give up on her other children. She went to churches and other groups of people, told her story and asked them to help her raise enough money to buy her other children out of slavery. After two years of speeches, fundraising, working, saving, and borrowing, Maria's mother bought the third brother. By the late 1850s, all her children were together and free. 🔳

Out of Alabama

John Thompson was sold three times in his life until finally, at 19 years old, he found himself in Huntsville, Alabama, owned by a young man who drank too much whiskey and, in John Thompson's words, "was always ready for a fight or a knock-down." He beat John so badly with a bullwhip that for three days John could not move his arm.

John decided to escape on a train. *On* the train. On *top of the* train. At sundown, he went to the tracks, watched for a northbound train, ran alongside, and latched on. Using the strength in his upper body, and pushing with his legs, John hauled himself up onto the roof of the train car. He traveled in this way all night.

William Still's report of John Thompson's story doesn't tell us many details about the trip itself. But the basic design of freight trains hasn't changed much since the 1850s. So we can easily imagine what it was like. Picture this:

He lies flat against the metal as the trail of choking coal exhaust rolls over and through him. He cannot sleep. He cannot slip. Nothing protects him from the rain or his fears or the slave catchers, who, unlike John Thompson, had the law on their side.

John Thompson grabbing hold to any bar or knob on the roof while the force of the train's slamming around curves and up and down hills threatened to slide his thin body over the sides. Tree branches tear over, scratching his face and raking his body. He lies flat against the metal as the trail of choking coal exhaust rolls over and through him. He cannot sleep. He cannot slip.

Nothing protects him from the rain or his fears or the slave catchers, who, unlike John Thompson, had the law on their side.

Then, just before dawn, John Thompson slips off the train car. He has to judge the speed of the train and the local terrain. He wants a wooded area, but not somewhere too thick for him to jump into. No doubt he looks for water to drink to keep himself alive. He's hungry, but food has to wait. Then he makes himself a nest in a thicket to hide in until morning and rest up for the next night's hazards.

Nowadays, a train from Philadelphia to Alabama takes about a day and a half. Done in nighttime sections like John Thompson was forced to make, the trip took two punishing weeks.

Worse yet, John Thompson didn't make it through.

In Virginia, between Richmond and Alexandria, he was captured on the ground. A young black man without papers back then was put into prison. His owner had advertised his escape in the papers. Virginia officers recognized him and sent word that he was found. So the young owner who drank whisky, and loved a fight and a knockdown, came up from Alabama to claim John Thompson and take him back to slavery.

John Thompson had no choice but to return. He stayed at his old place for a while, no doubt through severe punishments. He stayed while he was sold, for $1,300, to a trader. He stayed and did what he needed to do to stay alive.

~~~~~~

His will and determination curled up inside his slim young chest, waiting, watching through eyes that told nothing.

~~~~~~

But in his mind and heart, he did not stay. His spirit and imagination were on top of that railroad car, dangerous, cold, and uncomfortable as it was. His will and determination curled up inside his slim young chest, waiting, watching through eyes that told nothing.

Before he could be sold again, John Thompson took to the rails and made his way north again. This time, he used what he'd learned on his first, practice run up to Virginia. This time, he made it.

A few years later, William Still and the Underground Railroad Committee received a letter from John Thompson. He'd gone to New York, he said, and worked quite successfully as a barber until the trader found out where he was and came to the city to arrest him. Forced to run once more, John Thompson bought a one-way ticket—to London. This time he traveled *in*side. ◨

Woman Escaping in a Box

W e don't know her name, but we do know that in 1857, a young woman who was pregnant with her first child was determined to get away from the wealthy household in Baltimore where she was enslaved to work as a ladies' maid and seamstress. Babies born of mothers in bondage would be slaves, too. So the young woman was determined to get herself and her unborn child out of Baltimore so that the child could be born free. She and a young man named Thomas Shipley made a plan; then she watched for just the right chance to put it into action. It came on the day of the Grand Opening Ball at the Academy of Music, and everyone in the household was aflutter with preparations. They sent the young woman to buy a few last minute articles.

She kept on going.

When they realized she was missing, the young woman's owners questioned a free African-American woman whom they paid to wash their clothes. Because she could not—or would not—tell them where the young woman had gone, they fired her. They also offered a reward to anyone who could help them find the runaway. But no one said anything.

᭝᭝᭝

The two had come up with a plan to mail the young woman north as if she were a regular package of dry goods. Shipley had a large wooden box ready.

᭝᭝᭝

Meanwhile, the young woman met Thomas Shipley at a secret location.

Shipley was a wealthy young man who had already begun giving his money to help others. In this case, he became involved more directly. The two had come up with a plan to mail the young woman north as if she were a regular package of dry goods. Shipley had a large wooden box ready. He lined the bottom with clean straw. The young woman got in with her knees bent under her. Then he gave her a pair of scissors for her to use if she needed to make a hole to breathe.

No one has recorded what they said at that moment, if anything. So we do not know the nature of his fear or hers, or his encouragement. We do know that they went ahead with the plan. Shipley tucked more straw around her sides and over her head. Then, very carefully, he nailed the lid, drove the box to the Baltimore depot, and mailed the young woman care of the General Delivery in Philadelphia.

Once the box was paid for, Shipley traveled to Philadelphia, in order to arrive early and find someone who would pick it up the next day. Nice and regular—that was the point. It had to look like a normal business delivery.

The box was dark inside. No light. The air inside was choked with chaff from the straw. When packers came through to load the freight onto the railroad cars, they turned the young woman's box upside down more than once, throwing her onto her head and her side. When they went away, she worked to dig a tiny hole with the scissors Shipley had given her. Still, very little fresh air came in. She dared not cough or sneeze, and she hadn't drunk any water so that she would not have to urinate. She became thirsty and stiff. It was hard to breathe, hard to stay conscious, and so very dark and alone.

In Philadelphia, Thomas Shipley hired a man named George Custus to fetch the box. Custus was a deliveryman who owned a one-horse cart, called a dray, to take packages back and forth along the port, the railroad depot and businesses in the city. Shipley also arranged with an elderly lady, Mrs. Myers, to accept delivery.

Meanwhile, early in the morning, the young woman's box moved north with the rest of the mail on the railroad cars. She arrived in Philadelphia at 10 a.m. Although it was bright morning now and she was in a free state, inside the box she remained imprisoned in the dark.

 George Custus did not know what was in the box, but he judged from Shipley's worried face that whatever it was mattered a great deal. So Custus met the railroad car when it pulled into town. Before the train could be unloaded, Custus asked the conductor if he could go right into the railroad freight car and take out the box he'd been sent for. The conductor balked. He didn't like the idea of anyone taking mail out before it had been properly unloaded and inventoried, but Custus convinced him. He told the conductor that he needed to get this one to its destination immediately. And he reminded the conductor that he'd been coming to the depot every day for years. "You know me," he said. "I'll be responsible for the box."

"Take it," the conductor said, "and go ahead with it."

With great effort, Custus loaded the heavy box onto his dray and drove it to Mrs. Myers' house.

She had been waiting and she thought she was ready. Once the package was delivered to the row house at 412 South Seventh Street, however, once it sat in her house, silent and unmoving, the old lady got nervous. She hurried up the street to the house of her friend, Mrs. Ash, an undertaker. Mrs. Ash was used to dealing with dead bodies. Mrs. Myers hoped that the person in the box was alive, but she couldn't be sure.

Together they pried off the lid and saw the bulge of a human head and dark hair poking through the straw. The two women hesitated. One of them ventured a few words: "Get up, my child."

The woman in the box made a weak, tiny movement, just enough to rustle the surface of the straw. The two older women strained to help her straighten her body and climb stiffly out of the box. Then they led her upstairs to lie in a soft, clean bed.

All she could say was: "I feel so deadly weak."

In an hour or so, the women convinced her to drink some tea. Then she fell asleep. She slept that day and straight through the night. The next day she was able to talk a little more, but still with difficulty. On the third day she was able to sit up and talk. Soon after, the Vigilance Committee sent her on to freedom in Canada.

Before she left, the young woman tried to describe how afraid she'd been in the box, how alone, how real and suddenly close dying seemed. She couldn't explain, but maybe the wise old women understood, that once the box was tossed onto the platform, she was no longer a person, but a piece of mail, a box that could be dropped, left in the corner of a depot or a railroad car, knocked onto the rails, crushed under the weight of other freight loaded on top. She could not find words to say that the one night of imprisonment reflected her life of enslavement like a deadly magnifying glass: that all her life she'd been boxed in, really, moved around like an object, unable to draw a free breath on free soil, or bear children in the sunlight of liberty. What she did say they remembered and wrote down—that of all her fears the worst was that she'd be discovered and sent back to slavery. 🔲

~~~~

The two women hesitated. One of them ventured a few words: "Get up, my child."

~~~~

Salt Water Fugitive

Edward Davis was a drifter. As a boy and young man he'd gone to a school with his sister near Mother Bethel African Methodist Episcopal Church. They'd grown up in the "Cedar Ward," the old part of Philadelphia near the Delaware River where many east-west streets were named for trees: Walnut, Chestnut, Spruce, and Pine. Like many people in the Cedar Ward, Edward's sister lived and worked at the same place in the Cedar Ward for years. But for some reason, Edward could not seem to settle down.

Instead, he moved from one town to another, west through Pennsylvania to Harrisburg, and then south into Maryland, to Baltimore and Havre de Grace, where he worked the oyster boats. For a while he landed a job at a Maryland grocery store. It was a terrible mistake. Maryland had a law that most people didn't know about: free black people were *not allowed to come into the state.* Just being there, in other words, made Edward Davis a criminal. A constable who came into the grocery store saw Edward, didn't recognize him, questioned him and finding he was free, arrested him. All legal, and the worse was yet to come.

Laws that had been created to control free black people's movements hurt everyone. They kept black people enslaved. They kept free black people from enjoying rights that others took for granted. They made certain that both the free and enslaved black communities ended up doing millions of hours of work for which they never got paid. They kept the white population believing that the hateful system ought to be upheld—and made helping black people a crime. And they kept the U.S. from being as strong as it could have been and as true to its own Declaration of Independence.

But bad laws were made worse by the *outlaws* who used them to turn free people into instant money—legally. It was a scam, really, and here's how it worked: knowing that free black people who couldn't prove their freedom could be sold as slaves, kidnappers looked for men just like Edward—drifters and loners—to report to the courts. Without nearby family or friends to make a fuss, drifters could be arrested, no problem, and fined large amounts of money. When they couldn't pay their fines, the judge would make them stay in jail, or assign them to work to pay off the fines. And when the judge felt justified, or when he could get away with it, he might even sell someone into slavery to pay for his or her fines.

This is exactly what happened to Edward. And after months in jail, Edward was taken out, at 2:00 in the morning, and transported to Campbell's slave pen, a place where a "Negro trader" held people while he tried to sell them. Edward's job was to cook for the 60 people there; he thought that once he'd worked long enough and paid his fine, he'd be let free. Instead, in six months' time, Edward was shackled up and sent south, all the way to Savannah, Georgia.

In Savannah, Edward and two other men who were sold with him were put to work on the Possum Tail Railroad. It was a quaint name and killer work. Each week, he was given a basket of corn meal, four pounds of bacon, and a quart of molasses to eat. He had to cook his food the night before, wrap it in a rag, and take it with him to eat during the day. All the men on the railroad did the same. They got no fruit, no vegetables, no variety, and certainly not enough for a grown man working so hard that he had to be replaced every few months with somebody new. It's what the railroad did: they worked men like horses, and when some died, they bought new ones.

When Edward was broken, his owners transferred him to a cotton plantation. There the overseers almost finished him off. Finally, when he could no longer drag himself out to the fields, he was sent to a hospital for slaves. The two doctors said that his case of exhaustion was the worst they'd ever seen. In the 1800s they referred to men and women who'd been worked this way with the same word they used to describe horses whose strength had been used up: Edward's health had been broken. He lay in the hospital for two months before he was even able to walk again. When he did, his muscles remained so drawn up that one leg wouldn't straighten.

Terrified to be sent back to his killer-owner, Edward appealed to his doctors. As he told them his story, they noticed that he was an intelligent man with a Northern accent and education. In addition, his several jobs had made him a worker with many skills. The doctors offered to buy him from his owner, not to free him, but to work for them in the hospital. Even this, though still slavery, would have been better for Edward.

But his owner refused. As soon as Edward was well, he was to return to the plantation or the railroad, as he was needed. Edward knew that this time they would work him to death. Like so many others, then, Edward had nothing to lose.

In March of 1853, he ran away from the slave hospital and made his way to the port of Savannah. A cargo ship, the Keystone State, was loaded up and heading for Pennsylvania. Naturally, Edward had no money to bribe one of the sailors or the captain to let him on board. So he hauled himself up, bad leg and all, onto a ledge on the boat, up under the bow, where he could not be seen. He figured that his bottom half would get wet, but after all he'd been through, he figured he could take it. He held tight to the wooden beam that ran under the bow, every now and then fingering a hunk of bread he had stowed in his pocket. It wasn't much, but he figured that it would keep him alive until the Keystone State reached free land.

Edward hadn't realized that once the ship was under way, his broken body would plunge with the boat into and out of the waves. He held on. The temperature that March, which had been unseasonably mild, turned windy overnight and bitter cold. Freezing waves smashed into his body. He held his breath when the boat plunged him underwater and clamped himself onto the hull of the boat like a barnacle. It was all he could do. *Hold on.* The salt water stung and burned. When his head was above the water, he breathed deeply through shivers, just keeping alive until the next waves came crashing against him.

After 24 hours, Edward Davis was so frozen by the salt water and so exhausted from fighting the sea that he used the last breath in his body to call for the sailors to pull him on board. He knew that they'd turn him in, but at least he wouldn't slip into the ocean and become food or the sharks.

∿∿∿

After 24 hours, Edward Davis was so frozen by the salt water and so exhausted from fighting the sea that he used the last breath in his body to call for the sailors to pull him on board.

∿∿∿

For a while the sailors couldn't tell where the voice was coming from. No one had ever called from outside the boat, beneath the bow! When they finally found Edward, they threw him a rope. Somehow, he held on while they dragged him on deck. In the pocket of his wet jacket was a tiny pulp, which had once been the half a loaf of bread he hoped he'd eat on free soil.

The sailors took Edward below deck. They dried his body and gave him warm clothes. They fed him decent food and wrapped him in blankets. They were kind to the half-dead soul whom they fished out of the sea. But then the captain pulled the Keystone State into a Delaware port—and left Edward, barely walking, in a jailhouse there. The captain planned to deliver his own cargo in Philadelphia and then pick up Edward on the way back to be returned for a reward to his owner in Savannah.

Fortunately for Edward, the story of his escape and suffering came to the notice of a *Philadelphia Register* reporter. When abolitionists in Philadelphia read it, they contacted the Underground Railroad officers immediately, offering to buy Edward from his master and then set him free. What Edward needed instead, however, was money for a lawyer to help prove that he had indeed been a free man who'd once lived in House #5 on Steel's Court in the Cedar Ward in Philadelphia.

The Underground Railroad and the abolitionists found an excellent lawyer and paid his fee.

And although they rejoiced with Edward when he was restored to freedom, they knew that for the more than three million people he'd left behind in slavery there was not yet any legal way out of bondage. ▢

Ten Years in the Penitentiary for Owning *Uncle Tom's Cabin*

Like thousands of others, Rev. Green bought himself out of slavery. Although he'd never had formal education, he was a respected preacher in the Methodist church where he lived and worked first as a slave and then a free man in Indian Creek, Maryland. Rev. Green had a wife and a 25-year-old son, Sam, whom they'd not yet been able to buy free. But Sam didn't intend to wait. He'd met Harriet Tubman and he watched for an opportunity to escape along the route that she'd taken; and when it arose, he took it, heading straight north to Canada.

He'd met Harriet Tubman and he watched for an opportunity to escape along the route that she'd taken; and when it arose, he took it, heading straight north to Canada.

Within the year, Rev. Green decided to visit his son and see how he was doing in a new country, among new people. The old man was delighted to find that his son worked hard and loved God: these were the values that mattered most to the Reverend and his wife. It delighted him to see for himself that in Canada, no laws kept his son from building a full, rich life for himself and one day, for his own family. Rev. Green returned home to share his joy with his wife. Maybe because his own heart was not cluttered by hate, he failed to realize how much Sam's escape and his own trip had enraged the slave-owners in Indian Creek.

In fact, soon after Green's return, these men came to his house at night to search. What were they looking for? Anything they could find to use against him.

The men took Rev. Green's books, Sam's letters, maps of

Canada, and whatever they thought would prove that the mild and hard-working Rev. Green might be a threat. After two trials, the judge did indeed find cause to sentence Rev. Green to 10 years in prison. His crime: owning the best-known, best-loved, and worst-hated antislavery novel of the day—*Uncle Tom's Cabin,* which predicted the end of slavery.

His crime: owning the best-known, best-loved, and worst-hated antislavery novel of the day—*Uncle Tom's Cabin,* which predicted the end of slavery.

The elderly minister was shackled and sent to prison. In Maryland the government used prisoners to do work for the state as well as for businesses and farms. It was as if Rev. Green were enslaved all over again. For seven years of his ten-year sentence he labored, separate from Mrs. Green, unable to preach or enjoy the freedom he had worked so hard to purchase, or to visit his son.

Then, the prediction of *Uncle Tom's Cabin* came true. After a terrible Civil War, the legal system that had kept black people enslaved now freed them. And Rev. Green came home from prison.

Turpentine Stowaways

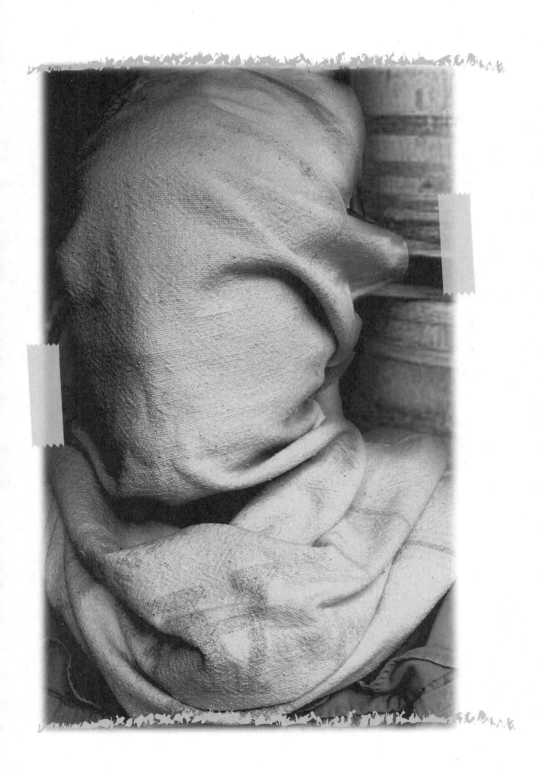

By the late 1850s as many as 100,000 people had escaped from slavery. And Southern states were trying everything to stop them. One idea that North Carolina's legislature made into law was this: The officers at each port were required to force smoke into the cargo compartments of all ships traveling north in order to choke out the stowaways. Even—or especially—captains who were in the habit of providing secret passage for fugitives couldn't get around the law.

Instead, the brave young men in their shrouds began to feel the effects of the ship's cargo: turpentine.

So when two young friends decided to hide on a ship leaving North Carolina, they sewed special sacks to protect them from the smoke. They called these shrouds, because they were like the covers used on dead bodies. But Abram Galloway and Richard Edons hoped that the sacks they'd made would be shrouds of life.

Each three-foot sack was cut from silk oilcloth. The plan was for them to slip the shrouds over their heads, and tie the drawstrings around their waists. Each young man would carry a bladder of water and towels, so that in case of heavy smoke, they could wet their towels and hold them over their noses to filter the worst of the smoky air.

At the exact minute they arrived at the wharf, the captain, who had agreed in advance to help, whisked them on in secret. But for some reason, whether through the captain's help or an officer's laziness or forgetfulness, this particular ship never got smoked.

Instead, the brave young men in their shrouds began to feel the effects of the ship's cargo: turpentine. Today we use turpentine as paint thinner and floor polish. Then, they used it for many purposes. Barrels and barrels of turpentine leaked toxic fumes, which Abram and Richard could not help but breathe in, despite the oilcloth. It came into their bodies, burning their eyes and noses and throats, burning tubes that carried air into their chests, and soon, causing a film of blood to leak from their pores like sweat. Inside the shrouds, they breathed through their moistened towels, bleeding and silent.

When they reached Philadelphia, they were very sick, but alive and happy. After a short recuperation, they traveled on to Canada, where they were finally safe from capture. Abram loved the simple privilege of going to work for money he got to keep for himself, and Richard soon opened his own shop.

In just a few years, when the Civil War began, Abram left his pleasant life in Canada to return to North Carolina to fight against slavery. He survived the war and remained in his home state. In just a few years, Abram Galloway, once a North Carolinian slave, was elected to the North Carolina State Senate. ⬒

∿∿∿

In just a few years, Abram Galloway, once a North Carolinian slave, was elected to the North Carolina State Senate.

∿∿∿

EPILOGUE

‿‿‿‿

By 1900, laws were enacted that made it nearly
impossible for the African-Americans in the South
to vote, own land, create wealth or acquire political power.

‿‿‿‿

Unfortunately, the story doesn't end there, in Abram Galloway's triumph. After the Civil War, and after the first stunning changes
to state and federal laws finally granting African-Americans the basic
rights of citizens, legislators in the South began working systematically
to reverse the laws that so many thousands had died for. By 1900, laws
were enacted that made it nearly impossible for the African-Americans
in the South to vote, own land, create wealth or acquire political power.
As in the days of slavery, the legal limitations were backed up by con-
stant legal and illegal force, beatings and killings, not only in the South,
but throughout the U.S. And beyond that, our books, newspapers, car-
toons and, later, movies, helped to reinforce the dangerous and untrue
idea that America would be safer and better if black people were kept
unequal and less free.

It was wrong, of course, and bad for the entire country, but
when the laws and outlaws and newspapers and books all said so, a lot
of people grew up believing it.

In the last 50 years, most of those laws have been changed. But what these courageous men and women knew is something that we also have to remember. We must pay attention to the rules by which we govern ourselves—and the history of how those laws came into being. This book is based on stories that were published in 1872, but largely ignored. The stories they told contradicted what the United States was telling itself and the world about its citizens of color.

These stories celebrate people who insisted on the American value of freedom. Moreover, the lives of people here show us that we have to work to *stay free* by refusing to ignore laws that enslave anyone among us and by electing people in state and federal government and courts who will make our society *more* free and *more* just. As they said in the 1800s: The price of freedom is eternal vigilance. 🔲

~·~·~·~

These stories celebrate people who insisted on the American value of freedom.

~·~·~·~